Yesterday House

YESTERDAY HOUSE

by Fritz Leiber

I

The narrow cove was quiet as the face of an expectant child, yet so near the ruffled Atlantic that the last push of wind carried the *Annie O.* its full length. The man in gray flannels and sweatshirt let the sail come crumpling down and hurried past its white folds at a gait made comically awkward by his cramped muscles. Slowly the rocky ledge came nearer. Slowly the blue V inscribed on the cove's surface by the sloop's prow died. Sloop and ledge kissed so gently that he hardly had to reach out his hand.

He scrambled ashore, dipping a sneaker in the icy water, and threw the line around a boulder. Unkinking himself, he looked back through the cove's high and rocky mouth at the gray-green scattering of islands and the faint dark line that was the coast of Maine. He almost laughed in satisfaction at having disregarded vague warnings and done the thing every man yearns to do once in his lifetime—gone to the farthest island out.

He must have looked longer than he realized, because by the time he dropped his gaze the cove was again as glassy as if the *Annie O.* had always been there. And the splotches made by his sneaker on the rock had faded in the hot sun. There was something very unusual about the quietness of this place. As if time, elsewhere hurrying frantically, paused here to rest. As if all changes were erased on this one bit of Earth.

The man's lean, melancholy face crinkled into a grin at the banal fancy. He turned his back on his new friend, the little green sloop, without one thought for his nets and specimen bottles, and set out to explore. The ground rose steeply at first and the oaks were close, but after a little way things went downhill and the leaves thinned and he came out on more

rocks—and realized that he hadn't quite gone to the farthest one
out.

*

Joined to this island by a rocky spine, which at the present low
tide would have been dry but for the spray, was another green,
high island that the first had masked from him all the while he
had been sailing. He felt a thrill of discovery, just as he'd
wondered back in the woods whether his might not be the first
human feet to kick through the underbrush. After all, there
were thousands of these islands.

Then he was dropping down the rocks, his lanky limbs now
moving smoothly enough.

To the landward side of the spine, the water was fairly still. It
even began with another deep cove, in which he glimpsed the
spiny spheres of sea urchins. But from seaward the waves
chopped in, sprinkling his trousers to the knees and making him
wince pleasurably at the thought of what vast wings of spray and
towers of solid water must crash up from here in a storm.

He crossed the rocks at a trot, ran up a short grassy slope,
raced through a fringe of trees—and came straight up against an
eight-foot fence of heavy mesh topped with barbed wire and
backed at a short distance with high, heavy shrubbery.

Without pausing for surprise—in fact, in his holiday mood,
using surprise as a goad—he jumped for the branch of an oak
whose trunk touched the fence, scorning the easier lower branch
on the other side of the tree. Then he drew himself up, worked
his way to some higher branches that crossed the fence, and
dropped down inside.

Suddenly cautious, he gently parted the shrubbery and, before
the first surprise could really sink in, had another.

A closely mown lawn dotted with more shrubbery ran up to a snug white Cape Cod cottage. The single strand of a radio aerial stretched the length of the roof. Parked on a neat gravel driveway that crossed just in front of the cottage was a short, square-lined touring car that he recognized from remembered pictures as an ancient Essex. The whole scene had about it the same odd quietness as the cove.

Then, with the air of a clock-work toy coming to life, the white door opened and an elderly woman came out, dressed in a long, lace-edged dress and wide, lacy hat. She climbed into the driver's seat of the Essex, sitting there very stiff and tall. The motor began to chug bravely, gravel skittered, and the car rolled off between the trees.

The door of the house opened again and a slim girl emerged. She wore a white silk dress that fell straight from square neck-line to hip-height waistline, making the skirt seem very short. Her dark hair was bound with a white bandeau so that it curved close to her cheeks. A dark necklace dangled against the white of the dress. A newspaper was tucked under her arm.

She crossed the driveway and tossed the paper down on a rattan table between three rattan chairs and stood watching a squirrel zigzag across the lawn.

*

The man stepped through the wall of shrubbery, called, "hello!" and walked toward her.

She whirled around and stared at him as still as if her heart had stopped beating. Then she darted behind the table and waited for him there. Granting the surprise of his appearance, her alarm seemed not so much excessive as eerie. As if, the man

7

thought, he were not an ordinary stranger, but a visitor from another planet.

Approaching closer, he saw that she was trembling and that her breath was coming in rapid, irregular gasps. Yet the slim, sweet, patrician face that stared into his had an underlying expression of expectancy that reminded him of the cove. She couldn't have been more than eighteen.

He stopped short of the table. Before he could speak, she stammered out, "Are you he?"

"What do you mean?" he asked, smiling puzzledly.

"The one who sends me the little boxes."

"I was out sailing and I happened to land in the far cove. I didn't dream that anyone lived on this island, or even came here."

"No one ever does come here," she replied. Her manner had changed, becoming at once more wary and less agitated, though still eerily curious.

"It startled me tremendously to find this place," he blundered on. "Especially the road and the car. Why, this island can't be more than a quarter of a mile wide."

"The road goes down to the wharf," she explained, "and up to the top of the island, where my aunts have a tree-house."

He tore his mind away from the picture of a woman dressed like Queen Mary clambering up a tree. "Was that your aunt I saw driving off?"

"One of them. The other's taken the motorboat in for supplies." She looked at him doubtfully. "I'm not sure they'll like it if they find someone here."

"There are just the three of you?" he cut in quickly, looking down the empty road that vanished among the oaks.

She nodded.

"I suppose you go in to the mainland with your aunts quite often?"

She shook her head.

"It must get pretty dull for you."

"Not very," she said, smiling. "My aunts bring me the papers and other things. Even movies. We've got a projector. My favorite stars are Antonio Morino and Alice Terry. I like her better even than Clara Bow."

He looked at her hard for a moment. "I suppose you read a lot?"

She nodded. "Fitzgerald's my favorite author." She started around the table, hesitated, suddenly grew shy. "Would you like some lemonade?"

*

He'd noticed the dewed silver pitcher, but only now realized his thirst. Yet when she handed him a glass, he held it untasted and said awkwardly, "I haven't introduced myself. I'm Jack Barry."

She stared at his outstretched right hand, slowly extended her own toward it, shook it up and down exactly once, then quickly dropped it.

He chuckled and gulped some lemonade. "I'm a biology student. Been working at Wood's Hole the first part of the summer. But now I'm here to do research in marine ecology—that's sort of sea-life patterns—of the in-shore islands. Under the direction of Professor Kesserich. You know about him, of course?"

She shook her head.

"Probably the greatest living biologist," he was proud to inform her. "Human physiology as well. Tremendous geneticist. In a class with Carlson and Jacques Loeb. Martin Kesserich—he lives over there at town. I'm staying with him. You ought to have heard of him." He grinned. "Matter of fact, I'd never have met you if it hadn't been for Mrs. Kesserich."

The girl looked puzzled.

Jack explained, "The old boy's been off to Europe on some conferences, won't be back for a couple days more. But I was to get started anyhow. When I went out this morning Mrs. Kesserich—she's a drab sort of person—said to me, 'Don't try to sail to the farther islands.' So, of course, I had to. By the way, you still haven't told me your name."

"Mary Alice Pope," she said, speaking slowly and with an odd wonder, as if she were saying it for the first time.

"You're pretty shy, aren't you?"

"How would I know?"

The question stopped Jack. He couldn't think of anything to say to this strangely attractive girl dressed almost like a "flapper."

"Will you sit down?" she asked him gravely.

The rattan chair sighed under his weight. He made another effort to talk. "I'll bet you'll be glad when summer's over."

"Why?"

"So you'll be able to go back to the mainland."

"But I never go to the mainland."

"You mean you stay out here all winter?" he asked incredulously, his mind filled with a vision of snow and frozen spray and great gray waves.

"Oh, yes. We get all our supplies on hand before winter. My aunts are very capable. They don't always wear long lace dresses. And now I help them."

"But that's impossible!" he said with sudden sympathetic anger. "You can't be shut off this way from people your own age!"

"You're the first one I ever met." She hesitated. "I never saw a boy or a man before, except in movies."

"You're joking!"

"No, it's true."

"But why are they doing it to you?" he demanded, leaning forward. "Why are they inflicting this loneliness on you, Mary?"

*

She seemed to have gained poise from his loss of it. "I don't know why. I'm to find out soon. But actually I'm not lonely. May I tell you a secret?" She touched his hand, this time with only the faintest trembling. "Every night the loneliness gathers in around me—you're right about that. But then every morning new life comes to me in a little box."

"What's that?" he said sharply.

"Sometimes there's a poem in the box, sometimes a book, or pictures, or flowers, or a ring, but always a note. Next to the notes I like the poems best. My favorite is the one by Matthew Arnold that ends,

'Ah, love, let us be true   To one another! for the world, which seems   To lie before us like a land of dreams,   So various, so beautiful, so new,   Hath really neither joy, nor love, nor light,   Nor certitude—'"

"Wait a minute," he interrupted. "Who sends you these boxes?"

"I don't know."

"But how are the notes signed?"

"They're wonderful notes," she said. "So wise, so gay, so tender, you'd imagine them being written by John Barrymore or Lindbergh."

"Yes, but how are they signed?"

She hesitated. "Never anything but 'Your Lover.'"

"And so when you first saw me, you thought—" He began, then stopped because she was blushing.

"How long have you been getting them?"

"Ever since I can remember. I have two closets of the boxes. The new ones are either by my bed when I wake or at my place at breakfast."

"But how does this—person get these boxes to you out here? Does he give them to your aunts and do they put them there?"

"I'm not sure."

"But how can they get them in winter?"

"I don't know."

"Look here," he said, pouring himself more lemonade, "how long is it since you've been to the mainland?"

"Almost eighteen years. My aunts tell me I was born there in the middle of the war."

"What war?" he asked startledly, spilling some lemonade.

"The World War, of course. What's the matter?"

Jack Barr was staring down at the spilled lemonade and feeling a kind of terror he'd never experienced in his waking life. Nothing around him had changed. He could still feel the same hot sun on his shoulders, the same icy glass in his hand, scent the same lemon-acid odor in his nostrils. He could still hear the faint *chop-chop* of the waves.

FRITZ LEIBER

And yet everything had changed, gone dark and dizzy as a landscape glimpsed just before a faint. All the little false notes had come to a sudden focus. For the lemonade had spilled on the headline of the newspaper the girl had tossed down, and the headline read:

HITLER IN NEW DEFIANCE
Under the big black banner of that head swam smaller ones:
Foes of Machado Riot in Havana
Big NRA Parade Planned
Balbo Speaks in New York

*

Suddenly he felt a surge of relief. He had noticed that the paper was yellow and brittle-edged.

"Why are you so interested in old newspapers?" he asked.

"I wouldn't call day-before-yesterday's paper old," the girl objected, pointing at the dateline: July 20, 1933.

"You're trying to joke," Jack told her.

"No, I'm not."

"But it's 1953."

"Now it's you who are joking."

"But the paper's yellow."

"The paper's always yellow."

He laughed uneasily. "Well, if you actually think it's 1933, perhaps you're to be envied," he said, with a sardonic humor he didn't quite feel. "Then you can't know anything about the Second World War, or television, or the V-2s, or Bikini bathing suits, or the atomic bomb, or—"

"Stop!" She had sprung up and retreated around her chair, white-faced. "I don't like what you're saying."

13

"But—"

"No, please! Jokes that may be quite harmless on the mainland sound different here."

"I'm really not joking," he said after a moment.

She grew quite frantic at that. "I can show you all last week's papers! I can show you magazines and other things. I can prove it!"

She started toward the house. He followed. He felt his heart begin to pound.

At the white door she paused, looking worriedly down the road. Jack thought he could hear the faint *chug* of a motorboat. She pushed open the door and he followed her inside. The small-windowed room was dark after the sunlight. Jack got an impression of solid old furniture, a fireplace with brass andirons.

"Flash!" croaked a gritty voice. "After their disastrous break day before yesterday, stocks are recovering. Leading issues...."

Jack realized that he had started and had involuntarily put his arm around the girl's shoulders. At the same time he noticed that the voice was coming from the curved brown trumpet of an old-fashioned radio loudspeaker.

The girl didn't pull away from him. He turned toward her. Although her gray eyes were on him, her attention had gone elsewhere.

"I can hear the car. They're coming back. They won't like it that you're here."

"All right they won't like it."

Her agitation grew. "No, you must go."

"I'll come back tomorrow," he heard himself saying.

"Flash! It looks as if the World Economic Conference may soon adjourn, mouthing jeers at old Uncle Sam who is generally referred to as Uncle Shylock."

Jack felt a numbness on his neck. The room seemed to be darkening, the girl growing stranger still.

"You must go before they see you."

"Flash! Wiley Post has just completed his solo circuit of the Globe, after a record-breaking flight of 7 days, 18 hours and 45 minutes. Asked how he felt after the energy-draining feat, Post quipped...."

*

He was halfway across the lawn before he realized the terror into which the grating radio voice had thrown him.

He leaped for the branch over-hanging the fence, vaulted up with the risky help of a foot on the barbed top. A surprised squirrel, lacking time to make its escape up the trunk, sprang to the ground ahead of him. With terrible suddenness, two steel-jawed semicircles clanked together just over the squirrel's head. Jack landed with one foot to either side of the sprung trap, while the squirrel darted off with a squeak.

Jack plunged down the slope to the rocky spine and ran across it, spray from the rising waves spattering him to the waist. Panting now, he stumbled up into the oaks and undergrowth of the first island, fought his way through it, finally reached the silent cove. He loosed the line of the *Annie O.*, dragged it as near to the cove's mouth as he could, plunged knee-deep in freezing water to give it a final shove, scrambled aboard, snatched up the boathook and punched at the rocks.

As soon as the *Annie O.* was nosing out of the cove into the cross waves, he yanked up the sail. The freshening wind filled it and sent the sloop heeling over, with inches of white water over the lee rail, and plunging ahead.

For a long while, Jack was satisfied to think of nothing but the wind and the waves and the sail and speed and danger, to have all his attention taken up balancing one against the other, so that he wouldn't have to ask himself what year it was and whether time was an illusion, and wonder about flappers and hidden traps.

When he finally looked back at the island, he was amazed to see how tiny it had grown, as distant as the mainland.

Then he saw a gray motorboat astern. He watched it as it slowly overtook him. It was built like a lifeboat, with a sturdy low cabin in the bow and wheel amidship. Whoever was at the wheel had long gray hair that whipped in the wind. The longer he looked, the surer he was that it was a woman wearing a lace dress. Something that stuck up inches over the cabin flashed darkly beside her. Only when she lifted it to the roof of the cabin did it occur to him that it might be a rifle.

But just then the motorboat swung around in a turn that sent waves drenching over it, and headed back toward the island. He watched it for a minute in wonder, then his attention was jolted by an angry hail.

Three fishing smacks, also headed toward town, were about to cross his bow. He came around into the wind and waited with shaking sail, watching a man in a lumpy sweater shake a fist at him. Then he turned and gratefully followed the dark, wide, fanlike sterns and age-yellowed sails.

II

The exterior of Martin Kesserich's home—a weathered white cube with narrow, sharp-paned windows, topped by a cupola—was nothing like its lavish interior.

In much the same way, Mrs. Kesserich clashed with the darkly gleaming furniture, persian rugs and bronze vases around her. Her shapeless black form, poised awkwardly on the edge of a huge sofa, made Jack think of a cow that had strayed into the drawing room. He wondered again how a man like Kesserich had come to marry such a creature.

Yet when she lifted up her little eyes from the shadows, he had the uneasy feeling that she knew a great deal about him. The eyes were still those of a domestic animal, but of a wise one that has been watching the house a long, long while from the barnyard.

He asked abruptly, "Do you know anything of a girl around here named Mary Alice Pope?"

The silence lasted so long that he began to think she'd gone into some bovine trance. Then, without a word, she got up and went over to a tall cabinet. Feeling on a ledge behind it for a key, she opened a panel, opened a cardboard box inside it, took something from the box and handed him a photograph. He held it up to the failing light and sucked in his breath with surprise.

It was a picture of the girl he'd met that afternoon. Same flat-bosomed dress—flowered rather than white—no bandeau, same beads. Same proud, demure expression, perhaps a bit happier.

"That is Mary Alice Pope," Mrs. Kesserich said in a strangely flat voice. "She was Martin's fiancee. She was killed in a railway accident in 1933."

YESTERDAY HOUSE

The small sound of the cabinet door closing brought Jack back to reality. He realized that he no longer had the photograph. Against the gloom by the cabinet, Mrs. Kesserich's white face looked at him with what seemed a malicious eagerness.

"Sit down," she said, "and I'll tell you about it."

Without a thought as to why she hadn't asked him a single question—he was much too dazed for that—he obeyed. Mrs. Kesserich resumed her position on the edge of the sofa.

"You must understand, Mr. Barr, that Mary Alice Pope was the one love of Martin's life. He is a man of very deep and strong feelings, yet as you probably know, anything but kindly or demonstrative. Even when he first came here from Hungary with his older sisters Hani and Hilda, there was a cloak of loneliness about him—or rather about the three of them.

"Hani and Hilda were athletic outdoor women, yet fiercely proud—I don't imagine they ever spoke to anyone in America except as to a servant—and with a seething distaste for all men except Martin. They showered all their devotion on him. So of course, though Martin didn't realize it, they were consumed with jealousy when he fell in love with Mary Alice Pope. They'd thought that since he'd reached forty without marrying, he was safe.

"Mary Alice came from a pure-bred, or as a biologist would say, inbred British stock. She was very young, but very sweet, and up to a point very wise. She sensed Hani and Hilda's feelings right away and did everything she could to win them over. For instance, though she was afraid of horses, she took up horseback riding, because that was Hani and Hilda's favorite pastime. Naturally, Martin knew nothing of her fear, and naturally his sisters knew about it from the first. But—and here is where Mary's wisdom fell short—her brave gesture did not pacify them: it only increased their hatred.

"Except for his research, Martin was blind to everything but his love. It was a beautiful and yet frightening passion, an insane cherishing as narrow and intense as his sisters hatred."

*

With a start, Jack remembered that it was Mrs. Kesserich telling him all this.

She went on, "Martin's love directed his every move. He was building a home for himself and Mary, and in his mind he was building a wonderful future for them as well—not vaguely, if you know Martin, but year by year, month by month. This winter, he'd plan, they would visit Buenos Aires, next summer they would sail down the inland passage and he would teach Mary Hungarian for their trip to Buda-Pesth the year after, where he would occupy a chair at the university for a few months ... and so on. Finally the time for their marriage drew near. Martin had been away. His research was keeping him very busy—"

Jack broke in with, "Wasn't that about the time he did his definitive work on growth and fertilization?"

Mrs. Kesserich nodded with solemn appreciation in the gathering darkness. "But now he was coming home, his work done. It was early evening, very chilly, but Hani and Hilda felt they had to ride down to the station to meet their brother. And although she dreaded it, Mary rode with them, for she knew how delighted he would be at her cantering to the puffing train and his running up to lift her down from the saddle to welcome him home.

"Of course there was Martin's luggage to be considered, so the station wagon had to be sent down for that." She looked defiantly at Jack. "I drove the station wagon. I was Martin's laboratory assistant."

She paused. "It was almost dark, but there was still a white cold line of sky to the west. Hani and Hilda, with Mary between them, were waiting on their horses at the top of the hill that led down to the station. The train had whistled and its headlight was graying the gravel of the crossing.

"Suddenly Mary's horse squealed and plunged down the hill. Hani and Hilda followed—to try to catch her, they said, but they didn't manage that, only kept her horse from veering off. Mary never screamed, but as her horse reared on the tracks, I saw her face in the headlight's glare.

"Martin must have guessed, or at least feared what had happened, for he was out of the train and running along the track before it stopped. In fact, he was the first to kneel down beside Mary—I mean, what had been Mary—and was holding her all bloody and shattered in his arms."

A door slammed. There were steps in the hall. Mrs. Kesserich stiffened and was silent. Jack turned.

The blur of a face hung in the doorway to the hall—a seemingly young, sensitive, suavely handsome face with aristocratic jaw. Then there was a click and the lights flared up and Jack saw the close-cropped gray hair and the lines around the eyes and nostrils, while the sensitive mouth grew sardonic. Yet the handsomeness stayed, and somehow the youth, too, or at least a tremendous inner vibrancy.

"Hello, Barr," Martin Kesserich said, ignoring his wife.

The great biologist had come home.

III

"Oh, yes, and Jamieson had a feeble paper on what he called individualization in marine worms. Barr, have you ever thought much about the larger aspects of the problem of individuality?"

Jack jumped slightly. He had let his thoughts wander very far.

"Not especially, sir," he mumbled.

The house was still. A few minutes after the professor's arrival, Mrs. Kesserich had gone off with an anxious glance at Jack. He knew why and wished he could reassure her that he would not mention their conversation to the professor.

Kesserich had spent perhaps a half hour briefing him on the more important papers delivered at the conferences. Then, almost as if it were a teacher's trick to show up a pupil's inattention, he had suddenly posed this question about individuality.

"You know what I mean, of course," Kesserich pressed. "The factors that make you you, and me me."

"Heredity and environment," Jack parroted like a freshman.

Kesserich nodded. "Suppose—this is just speculation—that we could control heredity and environment. Then we could re-create the same individual at will."

Jack felt a shiver go through him. "To get exactly the same pattern of hereditary traits. That'd be far beyond us."

"What about identical twins?" Kesserich pointed out. "And then there's parthenogenesis to be considered. One might produce a duplicate of the mother without the intervention of the male." Although his voice had grown more idly speculative, Kesserich seemed to Jack to be smiling secretly. "There are many examples in the lower animal forms, to say nothing of the technique by which Loeb caused a sea urchin to reproduce with no more stimulus than a salt solution."

Jack felt the hair rising on his neck. "Even then you wouldn't get exactly the same pattern of hereditary traits."

"Not if the parent were of very pure stock? Not if there were some special technique for selecting ova that would reproduce all the mother's traits?"

"But environment would change things," Jack objected. "The duplicate would be bound to develop differently."

"Is environment so important? Newman tells about a pair of identical twins separated from birth, unaware of each other's existence. They met by accident when they were twenty-one. Each was a telephone repairman. Each had a wife the same age. Each had a baby son. And each had a fox terrier called 'Trixie.' That's without trying to make environments similar. But suppose you did try. Suppose you saw to it that each of them had exactly the same experiences at the same times...."

For a moment it seemed to Jack that the room was dimming and wavering, becoming a dark pool in which the only motionless thing was Kesserich's sphinx-like face.

"Well, we've escaped quite far enough from Jamieson's marine worms," the biologist said, all brisk again. He said it as if Jack were the one who had led the conversation down wild and unprofitable channels. "Let's get on to your project. I want to talk it over now, because I won't have any time for it tomorrow."

Jack looked at him blankly.

"Tomorrow I must attend to a very important matter," the biologist explained.

IV

Morning sunlight brightened the colors of the wax flowers under glass on the high bureau that always seemed to emit the faint odor of old hair combings. Jack pulled back the diamond-patterned quilt and blinked the sleep from his eyes. He expected his mind to be busy wondering about Kesserich and his wife—things said and half said last night—but found instead that his thoughts swung instantly to Mary Alice Pope, as if to a farthest island in a world of people.

Downstairs, the house was empty. After a long look at the cabinet—he felt behind it, but the key was gone—he hurried down to the waterfront. He stopped only for a bowl of chowder and, as an afterthought, to buy half a dozen newspapers.

The sea was bright, the brisk wind just right for the *Annie O.* There was eagerness in the way it smacked the sail and in the creak of the mast. And when he reached the cove, it was no longer still, but nervous with faint ripples, as if time had finally begun to stir.

After the same struggle with the underbrush, he came out on the rocky spine and passed the cove of the sea urchins. The spiny creatures struck an uncomfortable chord in his memory.

This time he climbed the second island cautiously, scraping the innocent-seeming ground ahead of him intently with a boathook he'd brought along for the purpose. He was only a few yards from the fence when he saw Mary Alice Pope standing behind it.

He hadn't realized that his heart would begin to pound or that, at the same time, a shiver of almost supernatural dread would go through him.

YESTERDAY HOUSE

The girl eyed him with an uneasy hostility and immediately began to speak in a hushed, hurried voice. "You must go away at once and never come back. You're a wicked man, but I don't want you to be hurt. I've been watching for you all morning."

He tossed the newspapers over the fence. "You don't have to read them now," he told her. "Just look at the datelines and a few of the headlines."

When she finally lifted her eyes to his again, she was trembling. She tried unsuccessfully to speak.

"Listen to me," he said. "You've been the victim of a scheme to make you believe you were born around 1916 instead of 1933, and that it's 1933 now instead of 1951. I'm not sure why it's been done, though I think I know who you really are."

"But," the girl faltered, "my aunts tell me it's 1933."

"They would."

"And there are the papers ... the magazines ... the radio."

"The papers are old ones. The radio's faked—some sort of recording. I could show you if I could get at it."

"*These* papers might be faked," she said, pointing to where she'd let them drop on the ground.

"They're new," he said. "Only old papers get yellow."

"But why would they do it to me? *Why?*"

"Come with me to the mainland, Mary. That'll set you straight quicker than anything."

"I couldn't," she said, drawing back. "He's coming tonight."

"He?"

"The man who sends me the boxes ... and my life."

Jack shivered. When he spoke, his voice was rough and quick. "A life that's completely a lie, that's cut you off from the world. Come with me, Mary."

*

She looked up at him wonderingly. For perhaps ten seconds the silence held and the spell of her eerie sweetness deepened.

"I love you, Mary," Jack said softly.

She took a step back.

"Really, Mary, I do."

She shook her head. "I don't know what's true. Go away."

"Mary," he pleaded, "read the papers I've given you. Think things through. I'll wait for you here."

"You can't. My aunts would find you."

"Then I'll go away and come back. About sunset. Will you give me an answer?"

She looked at him. Suddenly she whirled around. He, too, heard the *chuff* of the Essex. "They'll find us," she said. "And if they find you, I don't know what they'll do. Quick, run!" And she darted off herself, only to turn back to scramble for the papers.

"But will you give me an answer?" he pressed.

She looked frantically up from the papers. "I don't know. You mustn't risk coming back."

"I will, no matter what you say."

"I can't promise. Please go."

"Just one question," he begged. "What are your aunts' names?"

"Hani and Hilda," she told him, and then she was gone. The hedge shook where she'd darted through.

Jack hesitated, then started for the cove. He thought for a moment of staying on the island, but decided against it. He could probably conceal himself successfully, but whoever found his boat would have him at a disadvantage. Besides, there were things he must try to find out on the mainland.

As he entered the oaks, his spine tightened for a moment, as if someone were watching him. He hurried to the rippling cove, wasted no time getting the *Annie O.* underway. With the wind still in the west, he knew it would be a hard sail. He'd need half a dozen tacks to reach the mainland.

When he was about a quarter of a mile out from the cove, there was a sharp *smack* beside him. He jerked around, heard a distant *crack* and saw a foot-long splinter of fresh wood dangling from the edge of the sloop's cockpit, about a foot from his head.

He felt his skin tighten. He was the bull's-eye of a great watery target. All the air between him and the island was tainted with menace.

Water splashed a yard from the side. There was another distant *crack*. He lay on his back in the cockpit, steering by the sail, taking advantage of what little cover there was.

There were several more *cracks*. After the second, there was a hole in the sail.

Finally Jack looked back. The island was more than a mile astern. He anxiously scanned the sea ahead for craft. There were none. Then he settled down to nurse more speed from the sloop and wait for the motorboat.

But it didn't come out to follow him.

V

Same as yesterday, Mrs. Kesserich was sitting on the edge of the couch in the living room, yet from the first Jack was aware of a great change. Something had filled the domestic animal with grief and fury.

"Where's Dr. Kesserich?" he asked.

"Not here!"

"Mrs. Kesserich," he said, dropping down beside her, "you were telling me something yesterday when we were interrupted."

She looked at him. "You *have* found the girl?" she almost shouted.

"Yes," Jack was surprised into answering.

A look of slyness came into Mrs. Kesserich's bovine face. "Then I'll tell you everything. I can now.

"When Martin found Mary dying, he didn't go to pieces. You know how controlled he can be when he chooses. He lifted Mary's body as if the crowd and the railway men weren't there, and carried it to the station wagon. Hani and Hilda were sitting on their horses nearby. He gave them one look. It was as if he had said, 'Murderers!'

"He told me to drive home as fast as I dared, but when I got there, he stayed sitting by Mary in the back. I knew he must have given up what hope he had for her life, or else she was dead already. I looked at him. In the domelight, his face had the most deadly and proud expression I've ever seen on a man. I worshiped him, you know, though he had never shown me one ounce of feeling. So I was completely unprepared for the naked appeal in his voice.

"Yet all he said at first was, 'Will you do something for me?' I told him, 'Surely,' and as we carried Mary in, he told me the rest. He wanted me to be the mother of Mary's child."

Jack stared at her blankly.

Mrs. Kesserich nodded. "He wanted to remove an ovum from Mary's body and nurture it in mine, so that Mary, in a way, could live on."

"But that's impossible!" Jack objected. "The technique is being tried now on cattle, I know, so that a prize heifer can have several calves a year, all nurtured in 'scrub heifers,' as they're called. But no one's ever dreamed of trying it on human beings!"

*

Mrs. Kesserich looked at him contemptuously. "Martin had mastered the technique twenty years ago. He was willing to take the chance. And so was I—partly because he fired my scientific imagination and reverence, but mostly because he said he would marry me. He barred the doors. We worked swiftly. As far as anyone was concerned, Martin, in a wild fit of grief, had locked himself up for several hours to mourn over the body of his fiancee.

"Within a month we were married, and I finally gave birth to the child."

Jack shook his head. "You gave birth to your own child."

She smiled bitterly. "No, it was Mary's. Martin did not keep his whole bargain with me—I was nothing more than his 'scrub wife' in every way."

"You *think* you gave birth to Mary's child."

Mrs. Kesserich turned on Jack in anger. "I've been wounded by him, day in and day out, for years, but I've never failed to recognize his genius. Besides, you've seen the girl, haven't you?"

Jack had to nod. What confounded him most was that, granting the near-impossible physiological feat Mrs. Kesserich had described, the girl should look so much like the mother. Mothers and daughters don't look that much alike; only identical twins did. With a thrill of fear, he remembered

Kesserich's casual words: "... parthenogenesis ... pure stock ... special techniques...."

"Very well," he forced himself to say, "granting that the child was Mary's and Martin's—"

"No! Mary's alone!"

Jack suppressed a shudder. He continued quickly, "What became of the child?"

Mrs. Kesserich lowered her head. "The day it was born, it was taken away from me. After that, I never saw Hilda and Hani, either."

"You mean," Jack asked, "that Martin sent them away to bring up the child?"

Mrs. Kesserich turned away. "Yes."

Jack asked incredulously, "He trusted the child with the two people he suspected of having caused the mother's death?"

"Once when I was his assistant," Mrs. Kesserich said softly, "I carelessly broke some laboratory glassware. He kept me up all night building a new setup, though I'm rather poor at working with glass and usually get burned. Bringing up the child was his sisters' punishment."

"And they went to that house on the farthest island? I suppose it was the house he'd been building for Mary and himself."

"Yes."

"And they were to bring up the child as his daughter?"

Mrs. Kesserich started up, but when she spoke it was as if she had to force out each word. "As his wife—as soon as she was grown."

"How can you know that?" Jack asked shakily.

The rising wind rattled the windowpane.

YESTERDAY HOUSE

"Because today—eighteen years after—Martin broke all of his promise to me. He told me he was leaving me."

VI

White waves shooting up like dancing ghosts in the Moon-sketched, spray-swept dark were Jack's first beacon of the island and brought a sense of physical danger, breaking the trancelike yet frantic mood he had felt ever since he had spoken with Mrs. Kesserich.

Coming around farther into the wind, he scudded past the end of the island into the choppy sea on the landward side. A little later he let down the reefed sail in the cove of the sea urchins, where the water was barely moving, although the air was shaken by the pounding of the surf on the spine between the two islands.

After making fast, he paused a moment for a scrap of cloud to pass the moon. The thought of the spiny creatures in the black fathoms under the *Annie O.* sent an odd quiver of terror through him.

The Moon came out and he started across the glistening rocks of the spine. But he had forgotten the rising tide. Midway, a wave clamped around his ankles, tried to carry him off, almost made him drop the heavy object he was carrying. Sprawling and drenched, he clung to the rough rock until the surge was past.

Making it finally up to the fence, he snipped a wide gate with the wire-cutters.

The windows of the house were alight. Hardly aware of his shivering, he crossed the lawn, slipping from one clump of shrubbery to another, until he reached one just across the drive from the doorway. At that moment he heard the approaching *chuff* of the Essex, the door of the cottage opened, and Mary Alice Pope stepped out, closely followed by Hani or Hilda.

Jack shrank close to the shrubbery. Mary looked pale and blank-faced, as if she had retreated within herself. He was acutely conscious of the inadequacy of his screen as the ghostly headlights of the Essex began to probe through the leaves.

But then he sensed that something more was about to happen than just the car arriving. It was a change in the expression of the face behind Mary that gave him the cue—a widening and side-wise flickering of the cold eyes, the puckered lips thinning into a cruel smile.

The Essex shifted into second and, without any warning, accelerated. Simultaneously, the woman behind Mary gave her a violent shove. But at almost exactly the same instant, Jack ran. He caught Mary as she sprawled toward the gravel, and lunged ahead without checking. The Essex bore down upon them, a square-snouted, roaring monster. It swerved viciously, missed them by inches, threw up gravel in a skid, and rocked to a stop, stalled.

*

The first, incredulous voice that broke the pulsing silence, Jack recognized as Martin Kesserich's. It came from the car, which was slewed around so that it almost faced Jack and Mary.

"Hani, you tried to kill her! You and Hilda tried to kill her again!"

The woman slumped over the wheel slowly lifted her head. In the indistinct light, she looked the twin of the woman behind Jack and Mary.

"Did you really think we wouldn't?" she asked in a voice that spat with passion. "Did you actually believe that Hilda and I would serve this eighteen years' penance just to watch you go off with her?" She began to laugh wildly. "You've never understood your sisters at all!"

Suddenly she broke off, stiffly stepped down from the car. Lifting her skirts a little, she strode past Jack and Mary.

Martin Kesserich followed her. In passing, he said, "Thanks, Barr." It occurred to Jack that Kesserich made no more question of his appearance on the island than of his presence in the laboratory. Like Mrs. Kesserich, the great biologist took him for granted.

Kesserich stopped a few feet short of Hani and Hilda. Without shrinking from him, the sisters drew closer together. They looked like two gaunt hawks.

"But you waited eighteen years," he said. "You could have killed her at any time, yet you chose to throw away so much of your lives just to have this moment."

"How do you know we didn't like waiting eighteen years?" Hani answered him. "Why shouldn't we want to make as strong an impression on you as anyone? And as for throwing our lives away, that was your doing. Oh, Martin, you'll never know anything about how your sisters feel!"

He raised his hands baffledly. "Even assuming that you hate me—" at the word "hate" both Hani and Hilda laughed softly—"and that you were prepared to strike at both my love and my work, still, that you should have waited...."

Hani and Hilda said nothing.

Kesserich shrugged. "Very well," he said in a voice that had lost all its tension. "You've wasted a third of a lifetime looking forward to an irrational revenge. And you've failed. That should be sufficient punishment."

Very slowly, he turned around and for the first time looked at Mary. His face was clearly revealed by the twin beams from the stalled car.

Jack grew cold. He fought against accepting the feelings of wonder, of poignant triumph, of love, of renewed youth he saw entering the face in the headlights. But most of all he fought against the sense that Martin Kesserich was successfully drawing them all back into the past, to 1933 and another accident. There was a distant hoot and Jack shook. For a moment he had thought it a railway whistle and not a ship's horn.

The biologist said tenderly, "Come, Mary."

*

Jack's trembling arm tightened a trifle on Mary's waist. He could feel *her* trembling.

"Come, Mary," Kesserich repeated.

Still she didn't reply.

Jack wet his lips. "Mary isn't going with you, Professor," he said.

"Quiet, Barr," Kesserich ordered absently. "Mary, it is necessary that you and I leave the island at once. Please come."

"But Mary isn't coming," Jack repeated.

Kesserich looked at him for the first time. "I'm grateful to you for the unusual sense of loyalty—or whatever motive it may have been—that led you to follow me out here tonight. And of course I'm profoundly grateful to you for saving Mary's life. But I must ask you not to interfere further in a matter which you can't possibly understand."

He turned to Mary. "I know how shocked and frightened you must feel. Living two lives and then having to face two deaths—it must be more terrible than anyone can realize. I expected this meeting to take place under very different circumstances. I wanted to explain everything to you very naturally and gently, like the messages I've sent you every day of your second life. Unfortunately, that can't be.

"You and I must leave the island right now."

Mary stared at him, then turned wonderingly toward Jack, who felt his heart begin to pound warmly.

"You still don't understand what I'm trying to tell you, Professor," he said, boldly now. "Mary is not going with you. You've deceived her all her life. You've taken a fantastic amount of pains to bring her up under the delusion that she is Mary Alice Pope, who died in—"

"She *is* Mary Alice Pope," Kesserich thundered at him. He advanced toward them swiftly. "Mary darling, you're confused, but you must realize who you are and who I am and the relationship between us."

"Keep away," Jack warned, swinging Mary half behind him. "Mary doesn't love you. She can't marry you, at any rate. How could she, when you're her father?"

"Barr!"

"Keep off!" Jack shot out the flat of his hand and Kesserich went staggering backward. "I've talked with your wife—your wife on the mainland. She told me the whole thing."

*

Kesserich seemed about to rush forward again, then controlled himself. "You've got everything wrong. You hardly deserve to be told, but under the circumstances I have no choice. Mary is not my daughter. To be precise, she has no father at all. Do you remember the work that Jacques Loeb did with sea urchins?"

Jack frowned angrily. "You mean what we were talking about last night?"

"Exactly. Loeb was able to cause the egg of a sea urchin to develop normally without union with a male germ cell. I have done the same tiding with a human being. This girl is Mary Alice Pope. She has exactly the same heredity. She has had exactly the same life, so far as it could be reconstructed. She's heard and read the same things at exactly the same times. There have been the old newspapers, the books, even the old recorded radio programs. Hani and Hilda have had their daily instructions, to the letter. She's retraced the same time-trail."

"Rot!" Jack interrupted. "I don't for a moment believe what you say about her birth. She's Mary's daughter—or the daughter of your wife on the mainland. And as for retracing the same time-trail, that's senile self-delusion. Mary Alice Pope had a normal life. This girl has been brought up in cruel imprisonment by two insane, vindictive old women. In your own frustrated desire, you've pretended to yourself that you've recreated the girl you lost. You haven't. You couldn't. Nobody could—the great Martin Kesserich or anyone else!"

Kesserich, his features working, shifted his point of attack. "Who are you, Mary?"

"Don't answer him," Jack said. "He's trying to confuse you."

"Who are you?" Kesserich insisted.

"Mary Alice Pope," she said rapidly in a breathy whisper before Jack could speak again.

"And when were you born?" Kesserich pressed on.

"You've been tricked all your life about that," Jack warned.

But already the girl was saying, "In 1916."

YESTERDAY HOUSE

"And who am I then?" Kesserich demanded eagerly. "Who am I?"

*

The girl swayed. She brushed her head with her hand.

"It's so strange," she said, with a dreamy, almost laughing throb in her voice that turned Jack's heart cold. "I'm sure I've never seen you before in my life, and yet it's as if I'd known you forever. As if you were closer to me than—"

"Stop it!" Jack shouted at Kesserich. "Mary loves me. She loves me because I've shown her the lie her life has been, and because she's coming away with me now. Aren't you, Mary?"

He swung her around so that her blank face was inches from his own. "It's me you love, isn't it, Mary?"

She blinked doubtfully.

At that moment Kesserich charged at them, went sprawling as Jack's fist shot out. Jack swept up Mary and ran with her across the lawn. Behind him he heard an agonized cry—Kesserich's—and cruel, mounting laughter from Hani and Hilda.

Once through the ragged doorway in the fence, he made his way more slowly, gasping. Out of the shelter of the trees, the wind tore at them and the ocean roared. Moonlight glistened, now on the spine of black wet rocks, now on the foaming surf.

Jack realized that the girl in his arms was speaking rapidly, disjointedly, but he couldn't quite make out the sense of the words and then they were lost in the crash of the surf. She struggled, but he told himself that it was only because she was afraid of the menacing waters.

He pushed recklessly into the breaking surf, raced gasping across the middle of the spine as the rocks uncovered, sprang to the higher ones as the next wave crashed behind, showering them with spray. His chest burning with exertion, he carried the girl the few remaining yards to where the *Annie O.* was tossing. A sudden great gust of wind almost did what the waves had failed to do, but he kept his footing and lowered the girl into the boat, then jumped in after.

She stared at him wildly. "What's that?"

He, too, had caught the faint shout. Looking back along the spine just as the Moon came clear again, he saw white spray rise and fall—and then the figure of Kesserich stumbling through it.

"Mary, wait for me!"

The figure was halfway across when it lurched, started forward again, then was jerked back as if something had caught its ankle. Out of the darkness, the next wave sent a line of white at it neck-high, crashed.

Jack hesitated, but another great gust of wind tore at the half-raised sail, and it was all he could do to keep the sloop from capsizing and head her into the wind again.

Mary was tugging at his shoulder. "You must help him," she was saying. "He's caught in the rocks."

He heard a voice crying, screaming crazily above the surf:

"Ah, love, let us be true

To one another! for the world—"

The sloop rocked. Jack had it finally headed into the wind. He looked around for Mary.

She had jumped out and was hurrying back, scrambling across the rocks toward the dark, struggling figure that even as he watched was once more engulfed in the surf.

Letting go the lines, Jack sprang toward the stern of the sloop.

But just then another giant blow came, struck the sail like a great fist of air, and sent the boom slashing at the back of his head.

His last recollection was being toppled out onto the rocks and wondering how he could cling to them while unconscious.

VII

The little cove was once again as quiet as time's heart. Once again the *Annie O.* was a sloop embedded in a mirror. Once again the rocks were warm underfoot.

Jack Barr lifted his fiercely aching head and looked at the distant line of the mainland, as tiny and yet as clear as something viewed through the wrong end of a telescope. He was very tired. Searching the island, in his present shaky condition, had taken all the strength out of him.

He looked at the peacefully rippling sea outside the cove and thought of what a churning pot it had been during the storm. He thought wonderingly of his rescue—a man wedged unconscious between two rock teeth; kept somehow from being washed away by the merest chance.

He thought of Mrs. Kesserich sitting alone in her house, scanning the newspapers that had nothing to tell.

He thought of the empty island behind him and the vanished motorboat.

He wondered if the sea had pulled down Martin Kesserich and Mary Alice Pope. He wondered if only Hani and Hilda had sailed away.

He winced, remembering what he had done to Martin and Mary by his blundering infatuation. In his way, he told himself, he had been as bad as the two old women.

He thought of death, and of time, and of love that defies them.

He stepped limpingly into the *Annie O.* to set sail—and realized that philosophy is only for the unhappy.

Mary was asleep in the stern.